W9-CZY-796

Katie Woo

Katie and the Fancy Substitute

by Fran Manushkin

illustrated by Tammie Lyon

PICTURE WINDOW BOOKS
a capstone imprint

Katie Woo is published by Picture Window Books
a Capstone Imprint
1710 Roe Crest Drive
North Mankato, Minnesota 56003
www.capstonepub.com

Text © 2015 Fran Manushkin
Illustrations © 2015 Picture Window Books

Library of Congress Cataloging-in-Publication Data
Manushkin, Fran, author.
  Katie and the fancy substitute / by Fran Manushkin; illustrated by
Tammie Lyon.
      pages cm. — (Katie Woo)
  Summary: There is an elegant substitute teacher in class today, but
Katie's attempts to impress her keep going wrong.
    ISBN 978-1-4795-5188-0 (hardcover) — ISBN 978-1-4795-5190-3 (pbk.)
    ISBN 978-1-4795-6157-5 (eBook)
1. Woo, Katie (Fictitious character)—Juvenile fiction. 2. Chinese
American children—Juvenile fiction. 3. Substitute teachers—Juvenile
fiction. 4. Elementary schools—Juvenile fiction. [1. Chinese Americans—
Fiction. 2. Substitute teachers—Fiction. 3. Schools—Fiction.] I. Lyon,
Tammie, illustrator. II. Title. III. Series: Manushkin, Fran. Katie Woo.

  PZ7.M3195Kaj 2014
  813.54—dc23   2013048930

Art Director: Heather Kindseth Wutschke
Graphic Designer: Kristi Carlson

Photo Credits:
Greg Holch, pg. 26
Tammie Lyon, pg. 26

Printed in the United States of America in Stevens Point, Wisconsin
032014   008092WZF14

Table of Contents

Chapter 1
Miss Bliss

Katie hurried to school.

She loved school, and

she loved her teacher, Miss

Winkle.

But Miss Winkle wasn't there.

"Good morning," said a new person. "Miss Winkle is sick today. I'll be your substitute. My name is Miss Bliss."

"Look at her jingly

bracelets," said Katie.

"And her sparkly shoes,"

whispered JoJo.

"Wow!" said

Katie. "Miss Bliss

is fancy."

"Oh, Miss Bliss," said Katie, "can I be your assistant today? I know everything."

"That's okay," said Miss Bliss. "I have lots of lesson plans."

"Let's start with math,"
she said. "Who can solve this
problem?"

"Me!" yelled Katie.

But Miss Bliss picked Pedro.
"Good work!" she praised
him.

"I knew
the answer,
too," sighed
Katie.

Miss Bliss picked Sophie

to lead the line to recess.

"Miss Bliss likes Sophie

because she's fancy," said

Katie. "Sophie sparkles."

After recess,
Katie said,
"Oh, Miss Bliss,
I have a fancy 
notebook. Can I show it to
you?"

"Not now," said Miss
Bliss. "It's time for silent
reading."

"I don't think Miss Bliss

likes me," said Katie. "I want

Miss Winkle back. I wish it

was tomorrow."

Chapter 2

Bam! Bling! Ring!

After lunch, Miss Bliss

said, "It's time for music.

Who wants to help pass out

the instruments?"

Katie raised her hand.

"You may do it," said

Miss Bliss.

"Yay!" Katie smiled. "Miss

Bliss finally picked me."

But Katie was so excited,

she dropped everything.

Bam! went the drums.

Bling! Ring! went the cymbals.

What a racket!

"Dopey girl," said Roddy.

Katie felt totally dopey.

The class began singing,
"Row, row, row your boat."
Sophie stood close to
Miss Bliss. She shook her
tambourine and her pretty
curls. Miss Bliss smiled at
her.

"I wish Miss Bliss would smile at me," said Katie.

Chapter 3
Katie's a Mess

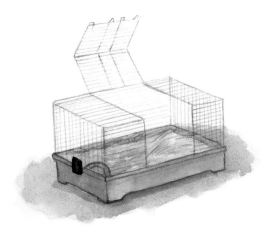

Next it was time for art.

Katie decided, "I'll paint

Binky. He always cheers

me up."

But Binky was gone!

Someone had opened his

cage.

Everyone looked for Binky.

Katie looked the hardest.

Whoops! She slipped on

some paint and fell down.

And that's when she

found Binky! He was

sleeping in the book basket

on top of *Harold and the*

Purple Crayon.

"Yay!" everyone cheered.

"Yech!" yelled Sophie.
"Katie is a mess! Her shirt is
stained, and she has paint
on her face. Katie should go
home right now!"

"Katie should stay right here," said Miss Bliss. "She is cheerful and helpful, and that is the best!"

"Really?" asked Katie. "Is that as good as fancy?"

"For sure!" said Miss Bliss. "Being your teacher is fun."

"Wow!" said Katie. "I can't wait to tell Miss Winkle!"

Miss Bliss smiled. "I think she already knows."

And she did!

About the Author

Fran Manushkin is the author of many popular picture books, including *Baby, Come Out!*; *Latkes and Applesauce: A Hanukkah Story*; *The Tushy Book*; *The Belly Book*; and *Big Girl Panties*. There is a real Katie Woo — she's Fran's great-niece — but she never gets in half the trouble of the Katie Woo in the books. Fran writes on her beloved Mac computer in New York City, without the help of her two naughty cats, Chaim and Goldy.

About the Illustrator

Tammie Lyon began her love for drawing at a young age while sitting at the kitchen table with her dad. She continued her love of art and eventually attended the Columbus College of Art and Design, where she earned a bachelor's degree in fine art. After a brief career as a professional ballet dancer, she decided to devote herself full time to illustration. Today she lives with her husband, Lee, in Cincinnati, Ohio. Her dogs, Gus and Dudley, keep her company as she works in her studio.

Glossary

assistant (uh-SISS-tuhnt)—a person who helps someone else do a task or job

bracelets (BRAYSS-lits)—bands worn around the wrist as pieces of jewelry

cymbals (SIM-buhls)—musical instruments made of brass and shaped like plates

jingly (JING-guh-lee)—making a tinkling or ringing sound

sparkles (SPAR-kuhls)—shines with many flashing points of light

substitute (SUHB-stuh-toot)—something or someone used in place of another

tambourine (tam-bur-EEN)—a small, round musical instrument that is similar to a drum. It has jingling metal disks around the rim and is played by shaking or striking it with the hand.

Discussion Questions

1. Why did Katie think that Miss Bliss didn't like her at the beginning of the story?

2. Do you think Katie had a good day or a bad day in this story? Explain your answer.

3. When Sophie said Katie was a mess, Katie felt sad. What would a good friend have said instead?

Writing Prompts

1. Pretend you are Katie and write a journal entry about your day with Miss Bliss.

2. Katie and JoJo think Miss Bliss is fancy. Why?

3. Think of a substitute teacher your class has had. How was the substitute similar to your teacher? How was he or she different?

Having Fun with Katie Woo!

Most of the class had a great time making music with Miss Bliss. You can make a tambourine to make music of your own! Here's how:

Tinkling Tambourine

What you need:

- 2 plain paper plates
- 2 pipe cleaners, each cut into fourths
- 8 jingle bells
- hole punch
- pencil
- markers

What you do:

1. Make 8 small marks around the end of a paper plate, about half an inch from the edge. Try to space them evenly.

2. Use the hole punch at each mark, punching through both paper plates.

3. Hold the plates so the top edges are together and the holes are lined up, creating an open space between the two plates.

4. Thread a jingle bell onto a piece of pipe cleaner. Then thread the pipe cleaner through a pair of holes. Twist the ends together and trim any extra pipe cleaner off. Repeat this process for all eight holes.

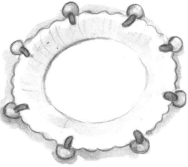

5. Use the markers to give your tambourine pizzazz!

Play along to music on the radio, or sing and dance on your own. Just be sure to shake that tambourine!

THE FUN DOESN'T STOP HERE!

Discover more at www.capstonekids.com

- ♥ Videos & Contests
- ✿ Games & Puzzles
- ♥ Friends & Favorites
- ✿ Authors & Illustrators

Find cool websites and more books like this one at www.facthound.com. Just type in the Book ID: 9781479551880 and you're ready to go!